BRAVE LITTLE BEAR

STEVE SMALL

A Paula Wiseman Book
Simon & Schuster Books for Young Readers
New York London Toronto Sydney New Delhi

SIMON & SCHUSTER BOOKS FOR YOUNG READERS
An imprint of Simon & Schuster Children's Publishing Division • 1230 Avenue of the Americas, New York, New York 10020 • © 2023 by Steve Small • Originally published in Great Britain in 2023 by Simon & Schuster UK Ltd. • Book design by Tom Daly © 2023 by Simon & Schuster, Inc. • All rights reserved, including the right of reproduction in whole or in part in any form. • SIMON & SCHUSTER BOOKS FOR YOUNG READERS and related marks are trademarks of Simon & Schuster, Inc. • For information about special discounts for bulk purchases, please contact Simon & Schuster Special Sales at 1-866-506-1949 or business@simonandschuster.com. • The Simon & Schuster Speakers Bureau can bring authors to your live event. For more information or to book an event, contact the Simon & Schuster Speakers Bureau at 1-866-248-3049 or visit our website at www.simonspeakers.com. • The text for this book was set in Aleo. • Manufactured in China • 0623 SUK • First US Edition • 1 2 3 4 5 6 7 8 9 10 • CIP data for this book is available from the Library of Congress. • ISBN 9781665951104 • ISBN 9781665951111 (ebook)

For Mum

It was early morning, and three bears were fast asleep in their cave.

Arlo was the first to wake.

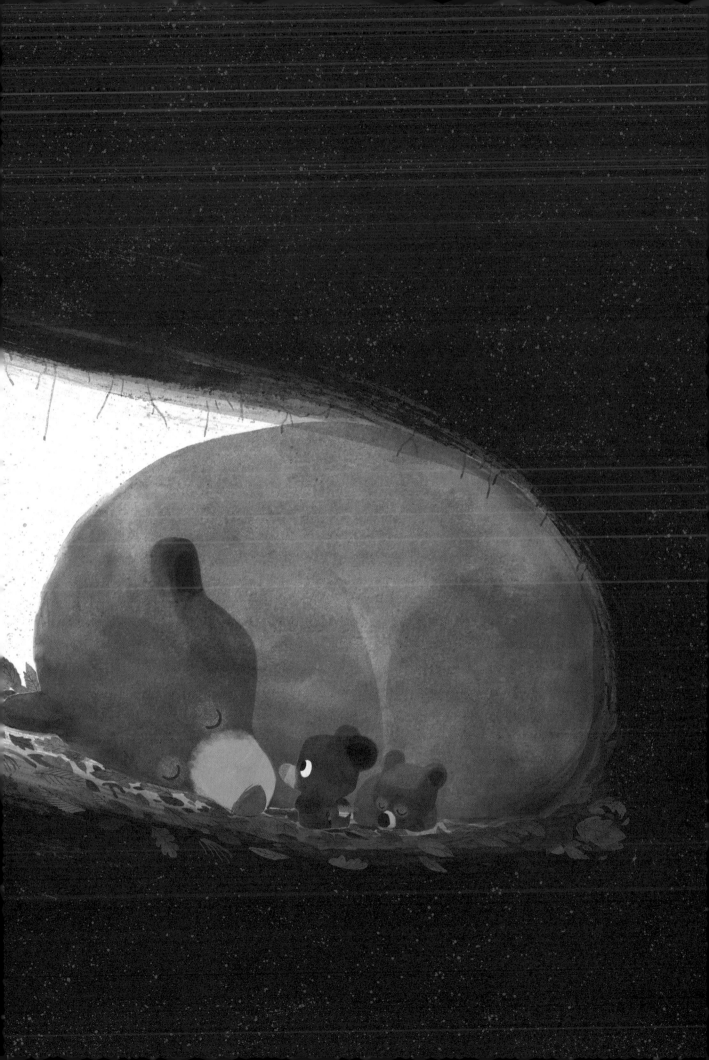

As soon as his sister, Eva, began to stir, she was eager to start the day. To her, the world was full of new things to discover.

But Arlo liked things just as they were.

He liked the warmth of their den where they all slept.

He liked how there was not quite enough room.

He even liked it when their snores woke him
up in the night . . .

because he'd get to curl up and fall asleep
next to Eva and his mother all over again.

But all this was about to change. Today they were going to leave the only home Arlo had ever known.

Winter was nearly over, and it was time to leave the mountain and go to live in Spring Valley.

"It'll be an adventure!" their mother had said.

Arlo knew what adventures meant. More new things.

As Arlo watched Eva play outside,
their mother whispered
into his ear.

"Follow me,
my brave
little bear,"
she said.

Arlo took one last
look around the den.
I wish I were brave,
he thought to himself.

They set off into the Great Wood, where their mother had taught them how to be grown-up bears.

Eva had been first up that tree.

First down that steep hill.

And first in the water.

She didn't seem to be afraid of anything.
Eva is the brave one,
Arlo thought.

"Arlo! Look!" said Eva.
A tall mountain ridge covered
in snow stood before them.

A cold wind began to blow.

Their mother looked at them both carefully and said, "Spring Valley is on the other side. We need to cross."

They began to climb the slope,
Eva running ahead.

The wind blew harder.

"Stay close!"
their mother said sharply.

Suddenly . . .

the world disappeared.

A huge snowstorm blew across the mountain.

Arlo pressed as tightly as he
could to their mother's
side as she concentrated
on each step.

But even though he could hardly see in front of him, Arlo knew Eva wasn't nearby.

Something was wrong.

Arlo quickly turned and looked behind him. Though the wind blew loudly, he was *sure* he had heard something.

There!

Again!

It was getting farther away.

Arlo's eyes grew wide—
he knew that sound.

It was Eva.

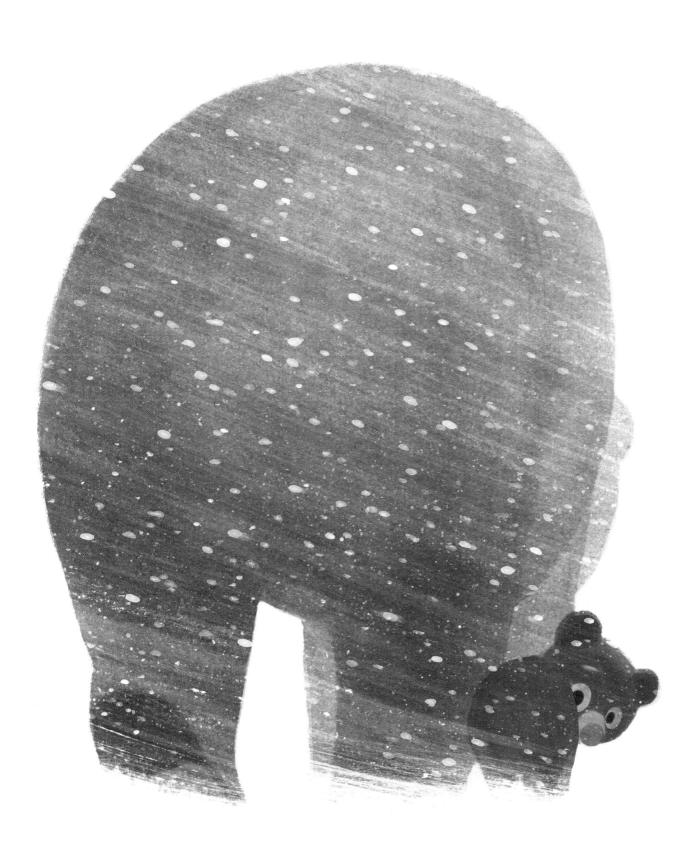

Eva had been sure she was only a few steps in front when the storm came.

She had used all her courage to walk back to find her brother and mother.

But now she had no idea where she was.

"ARLO!" she cried again. But the wind was so strong, she could barely hear herself.

She couldn't take another step. Then, as Eva drew breath for another cry, she held it for a moment. Had she just seen something in the distance?

No. There was nothing. They must be far away by now. It was impossible.

Then the impossible . . . happened.

Out of the storm, Arlo ran toward her.

"...ARLO!"

Arlo pressed close to his sister.
He couldn't believe he had found her.
"Arlo! Arlo! You're here!
I'm so lost. I'm so afraid!"

Arlo hadn't had a chance to feel fear when he had set out to find Eva. He had just run without thinking.

But now it was different.
"Yes." He nodded. "I'm afraid too."

Then Arlo remembered what his mother had said when he had first felt afraid that morning: "Follow me, my brave little bear."

Arlo looked at Eva and realized that this time it was *his* turn to be brave.

They turned to face the storm, and Arlo wondered
how they could possibly know which way to go.

And that was when he saw them . . .

a few deep prints from their mother's long stride.
They were on the right path!

"This way, Eva," cried Arlo.

It was a long, hard journey.

Often the marks in the snow were
nowhere to be seen.

And sometimes they would climb and climb . . .

and slide all the way back down again.

But every time, they got back on their feet
and carried on.

And just when it seemed as if the storm
would never end . . .

it stopped.

They could smell Spring Valley before they could see it. A faint breeze blew, and they could almost taste the flowers and feel the warmth of the sun on their fur.

They had made it over the ridge.

And there, not many more steps away,
eyes desperately searching the mountainside,
stood their mother.

"WE'RE HERE!

WE'RE HERE!"

Eva and Arlo cried.

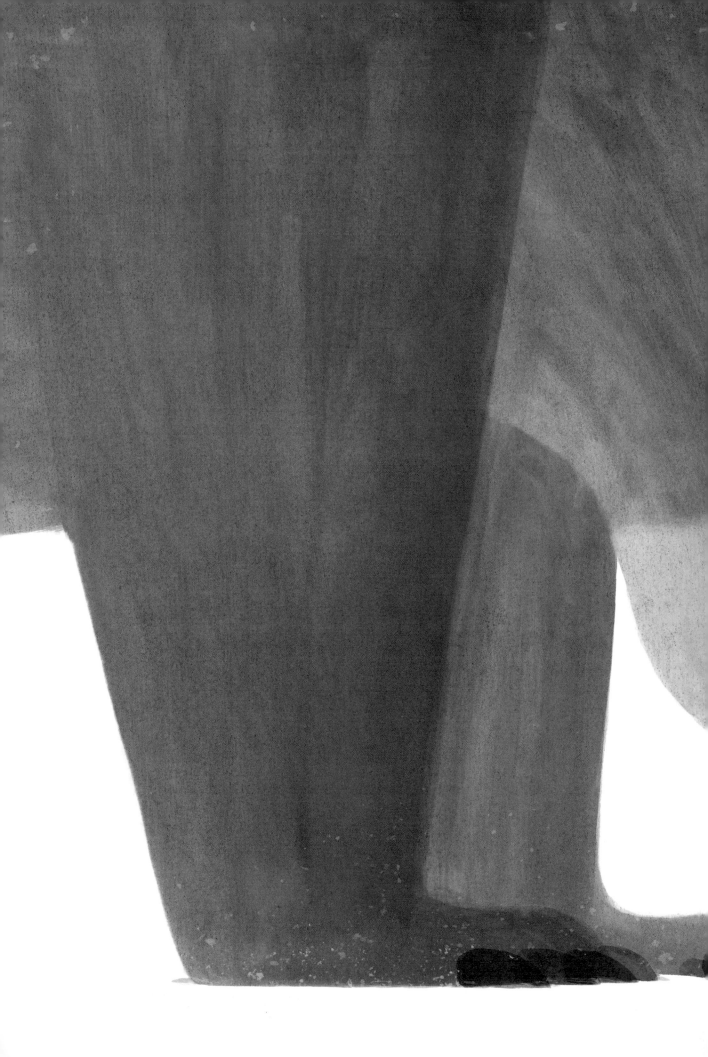

She bounded toward them,
happy and scolding at the same
time, but her words were soft.

"I was so worried!" she said.
"We were so afraid," said Eva.
"But we did try to be brave!"
added Arlo.

Their mother looked at them
both with her serious, gentle eyes.
"Being brave when you feel afraid,"
she said, "is the very bravest brave of all."

Later that night, sleeping under the moon,
Arlo woke to the sound of his sister's and
mother's snores . . .

and with a dreamy smile, he growled
happily, curled up, and fell back to sleep.